CREAM OF CREATURE
FROM THE
SCHOOL CAFETERIA

by Mike Thaler

Illustrated by
Jared Lee

A Snuggle & Read Story Book

AN AVON CAMELOT BOOK

This book is dedicated to
Mrs. Gelé's
6th grade class of 1982
at
Osborne Elementary School
New Orleans, Louisiana
for all their help and inspiration

AVON BOOKS
A division of
The Hearst Corporation
105 Madison Avenue
New York, New York 10016

Library of Congress Cataloging in Publication Data

Thaler, Mike, 1936–
    Cream of creature from the school cafeteria.

    (A Snuggle & read story book) (An Avon Camelot book)
    Summary: When the food in the school cafeteria takes
on a life of its own and spreads out as a green blob
eating everything in sight, the students find there is
only one way to stop it.
    [1. Monsters—Fiction. 2. Schools—Fiction]
I. Lee, Jared D., ill. II. Title. III. Series.
IV. Series: Avon Camelot book.
PZ7.T3Cr 1985   [Fic]   85-47644

First Camelot Printing, October 1985

Printed in the U.S.A.

BAN 10 9 8 7 6

It was lunchtime.

Our class walked slowly toward the cafeteria, holding our noses.

We could smell the food
all the way down the hall.
It was also making funny noises.

We opened the cafeteria door.
We took our trays
and were about to line up...
when we backed away from
the lunch counter in horror!

The food was moving!!
It burbled and glurped in the pans.

Then it slurped out of the pans,
over the side of the counter,
and across the cafeteria floor.
It was coming at us!!!

We threw our lunch trays in the air
and ran out the door.

Mrs. Crumb, the cook, ran out of the cafeteria, shouting at the food.
She tried to hit it with a serving spoon.

The food blurped over her white shoes,
and she was gone.

We ran into the main office.
"Call the sheriff, call the sheriff!" we all shouted.
"*Now* what's wrong?"
said Mrs. Bagley, the principal.

"The food is after us!" we screamed.
"Now, now," said Mrs. Bagley,
opening the office door and stepping out.
"There's absolutely nothing to..." GLURP!

She never finished her sentence—
she just disappeared into the bubbling green.

We ran into her office and locked the door.
Through the glass we could see the food
eating all the safety posters.

We dialed the sheriff.
Soon we heard his siren.

He burst in, took out his gun,
and told the food not to move.
The food moved.
He shot three bullets at it.
"Blup, blup, blup!"
The food liked the bullets.
It happily burbled and chased the sheriff
all the way out of the school.

We dialed the fire department.
A big red engine roared up.
The food was eating the flagpole.
The firemen unrolled a huge hose
and squirted the food with water.
The food splashed merrily and took a bath.

We dialed the army.

A jeep pulled up.

Four soldiers jumped out with flame throwers.

They turned the flames on the food.

The food warmed up, it bubbled over their boots, and they were all eaten by a *hot lunch!*

We dialed the air force.
Soon two jet planes roared overhead.

The pilots spotted the food heading for our jungle gym.
They each dropped a bomb on the food.
But the food just burped, then ate the jungle gym, the slides, and all our swings.
We all screamed.

Then we thought of Mickey.
"Mickey is the only one who can save us.
Mickey will eat anything!"

We found Mickey licking the snack machine.
We told him what had happened.
He smiled.

He walked calmly to the center of the
playground.
He sat down in front of the food—
and took out two spoons.

The food burbled, and out came Mrs. Crumb.

The food burbled again,
and out came Mrs. Bagley.

The food burbled a third time, and out came
the safety posters and the soldiers.

The food looked at Mickey.
Mickey looked at the food.
It burbled and glurped and slithered toward him.
Closer...Closer...

Mickey's spoons flashed in the sunlight, and...

HE ATE IT!
HE ATE IT ALL!!
HE ATE IT ALL UP!!!

Then he licked his spoons,
twirled them, put them back in his pockets,
and asked for seconds.

We all cheered.

The mayor came.
He gave Mickey a bright medal for saving
the school.

Mickey looked at the medal,
smiled,

and ate it.